MW00917175

This Books

Belongs To

Made in the USA
Las Vegas, NV
24 August 2021

28812638R00059